5025   LIBRARY
ANDERSON ELEMENTARY SCHOOL

T5-AQQ-640

UNCLE SAM AND THE FLAG

Written by

Dr. Lee Mountain

Illustrated by

Jeanne Pearson

published by

ODDO PUBLISHING

Fayetteville, Georgia

Symbol for exciting book ideas

5025
ANDERSON ELEMENTARY SCHOOL LIBRARY

Dedicated to

my family

Read, Explore, and Develop

Copyright © 1978 by ODDO PUBLISHING, INC., Fayetteville, Georgia 30214

ALL RIGHTS RESERVED. No part of this book may be used or reprinted in any manner
whatsoever without the written permission of the publisher.
Library of Congress Catalog Number 77-83633
ISBN 0-87783-145-9
Printed in the United States of America

"What do boys and girls mean
By the words they say
When they talk to the flag
Of the U.S.A.?"

"Talk to the flag?
That is not what they do.
They pledge allegiance,
And so can you."

"We pledge allegiance?
But we are just birds.
Uncle Sam, we do not
Even know the words."

5

"I will say the Pledge
All the way through,
And I will explain
What it means to you.

"I pledge allegiance
To the flag
Of the United States
Of America
And to the republic
For which it stands,
One nation
Under God,
Indivisible,
With liberty
And justice for all."

"*Pledge* is a word
I never have seen.
And tell me, what
Does *allegiance* mean?"

"To pledge means to promise —
Just what you will do.
When you promise allegiance
You pledge to be true.

9 5025
ANDERSON ELEMENTARY SCHOOL LIBRARY

"When pledging allegiance
We always stand
To show that we love
And respect our land."

"You know, I think
That I have guessed
Why you say the Pledge
With your hand on your chest.
You take this position
Before your start
To show that the words
Come right from your heart."

"Because of the things
You have taught us today,
We always will know
What we mean when we say:

"I pledge allegiance
To the flag
Of the United States
Of America."

"I will teach you more.
  Cover hearts with hands.
    And to the republic
    For which it stands."

"The republic, Uncle Sam?
What could that be?
The word, *republic*,
Is new to me."

"I learned that word
  From the owl in the steeple.
Republic means government
By the people.

17

"The people can vote
So they can direct
The men and women
That they elect.
Yes, all of the voters
Can have a say
In the government
On Election Day.

"When pledging, we say
We are faithful and true,
Not just to our flag,
But to our people, too."

"Now that I understand
  All of that part,
I can say half
Of the Pledge by heart:

"I pledge allegiance
To the flag
Of the United States
Of America
And to the republic
For which it stands."

"The rest is not hard
To understand.
The rest of the Pledge
Describes our land:

"One nation
Under God,
Indivisible,
With liberty
And justice
For all.

"You see, it contains
Just one long word
That might be hard
To explain to a bird."

"Yes, *indivisible*.
What in creation
Is meant by an
Indivisible nation?"

"It's a grouping of states
That right from the start
Could not be divided
And broken apart.

"The end of the Pledge
Is saying to you
That you will have justice
And liberty, too.

"Justice for all
   Means fairness, you see.
   And liberty means
   You will always be free."

"We understand the Pledge
All the way through.
So now we can say it
By heart for you:

"I pledge allegiance
To the flag
Of the United States
Of America
And to the republic
For which it stands,
One nation
Under God,
Indivisible,
With liberty
And justice
For all."

about the author

DR. LEE MOUNTAIN, the author of UNCLE SAM AND THE FLAG, is a professor in the College of Education, University of Houston, Texas. She has written more than thirty other books for children and adults.

She and her husband, Dr. Joseph Mountain, have four children whose nicknames go well with their surname — Candy, Smoky, Cliff, and Rocky.

As these four children started school and learned the Pledge of Allegiance, their mother came to realize that memorizing the words was not enough. They needed to comprehend the meaning behind the words.

Comprehension of the Pledge posed a problem for many primary pupils, according to the teachers with whom Dr. Mountain worked. These teachers said their children needed an easy-to-read book explaining the hard-to-understand words in the Pledge.

So Dr. Mountain wrote UNCLE SAM AND THE FLAG — so that children who say, "I pledge allegiance..." can know what they are talking about.

about the illustrator

JEANNE PEARSON is a graduate of Winona State College with majors in Art and English. When she is not illustrating and writing children's books, Jeanne does paintings of the North American big game animals and of horses. She has taken numerous trips out West to gain background material for her paintings and for the books she has done on the American Indian.

Jeanne and her husband, Charles, have four daughters. They live on a farm in Stewartville, Minnesota, where they raise registered Appaloosa horses.

UNCLE SAM AND THE FLAG is the sixth publication Jeanne has illustrated for Oddo Publishing. Other Oddo titles in which she has had a hand include ADVENTURES ON LIBRARY SHELVES, LITTLE INDIANS' ABC, DIPS 'N' DOODLES, WHISPERING RIVER, and KEIKI OF THE ISLANDS.